Dear Parent:
Your child's love of reading starts here!

Every child learns to read in a different way and at his or her own speed. Some go back and forth between reading levels and read favorite books again and again. Others read through each level in order. You can help your young reader improve and become more confident by encouraging his or her own interests and abilities. From books your child reads with you to the first books he or she reads alone, there are I Can Read Books for every stage of reading:

SHARED READING
Basic language, word repetition, and whimsical illustrations, ideal for sharing with your emergent reader

BEGINNING READING
Short sentences, familiar words, and simple concepts for children eager to read on their own

READING WITH HELP
Engaging stories, longer sentences, and language play for developing readers

READING ALONE
Complex plots, challenging vocabulary, and high-interest topics for the independent reader

ADVANCED READING
Short paragraphs, chapters, and exciting themes for the perfect bridge to chapter books

I Can Read Books have introduced children to the joy of reading since 1957. Featuring award-winning authors and illustrators and a fabulous cast of beloved characters, I Can Read Books set the standard for beginning readers.

A lifetime of discovery begins with the mag

Visit www.icanread.com for in
on enriching your child's reading

D1530622

I Can Read!

READING 2 WITH HELP

FLICKA
A Friend for Katy

Novelization by JENNIFER FRANTZ

Based on the motion picture

screenplay by MARK ROSENTHAL &

LAWRENCE KONNER

Based on the novel "My Friend Flicka" by

MARY O'HARA

HarperCollins *Publishers*

FOX 2000 PICTURES PRESENTS A GIL NETTER PRODUCTION "FLICKA" ALISON LOHMAN TIM McGRAW MARIA BELLO
COSTUME DESIGNER MOLLY MAGINNIS MUSIC SUPERVISOR JASON ALEXANDER MUSIC BY AARON ZIGMAN CO-PRODUCER KEVIN HALLORAN FILM EDITOR ANDREW MARCUS
PRODUCTION DESIGNER SHARON SEYMOUR DIRECTOR OF PHOTOGRAPHY J. MICHAEL MURO PRODUCED BY GIL NETTER BASED UPON THE NOVEL "MY FRIEND FLICKA" BY MARY O'HARA
SCREENPLAY BY MARK ROSENTHAL & LAWRENCE KONNER DIRECTED BY MICHAEL MAYER
www.flickamovie.com

© 2005 Twentieth Century Fox

Flicka: A Friend for Katy
Flicka ™ & © 2006 Twentieth Century Fox Film Corporation.
All rights reserved. Printed in the United States of America.
No part of this book may be used or reproduced in any manner whatsoever without written permission except in the case of brief
quotations embodied in critical articles and reviews. For information address HarperCollins Children's Books, a division of
HarperCollins Publishers, 1350 Avenue of the Americas, New York, NY 10019.
www.icanread.com
Library of Congress Catalog card number: 2005017662
ISBN-10: 0-06-087609-3—ISBN-13: 978-0-06-087609-8
Typography by Scott Richards

1 2 3 4 5 6 7 8 9 10   ❖   First Edition

Some say the history of the American West was written by the horse. Katy McLaughlin believed that with all her heart.

Horses were in her blood.

Katy's family owned a ranch in the
Neversummer Mountains of Wyoming.
One day she went for a bareback ride.
A mountain lion scared her horse,
and he flung her off his back.

Katy ran for her life,

with the lion right behind her.

She emerged from the trees,

and startled a beautiful black filly

grazing in a field.

When the horse saw the lion,

she reared and struck out.

The lion ran away.

So did the black filly.

Katy stared after her in wonder.

She didn't know there were any

mustangs on the ranch. . . .

Katy ran home as fast as she could.
"A lion!" she told her father.
"Right there in front of me . . .
and a horse—a *mustang*!"
That meant she was a wild,
untamed horse.

Her father did not like mustangs.
He said they ate up his pasture.

But Katy wanted to see
the black filly again.
She rode out into the wilderness
searching for her.
There she was!
Katy's grip tightened on the rope
she held.

Katy was a good roper.

She threw the loop and

caught the wild horse.

But the filly was stronger

than she expected.

She jumped and spun,

dragging Katy from the saddle.

The mustang filly ran.

Katy skidded along behind her,

trying desperately to hold on.

But it was no use.

The filly broke away,

spooking the herd.

Katy's father was angry
at the mustang for
scattering his horses.
He said the horse was *loco*—crazy.
He caught the mustang
and put her in the round pen alone.

"She will calm down
once I start training her," Katy said.
But her father did not want her
to try to ride the filly.
"This is a dangerous animal,"
he told Katy.

But Katy knew the black filly was special.

She named her Flicka.

She sneaked out to see her
in the round pen.

At first, Flicka charged her
when she tried to enter the pen.

But soon Flicka began to trust Katy.
Katy fed her apples and taught her
to accept a blanket on her back.

She taught her to wear a halter.

There was just one more thing to do.

Katy made sure the filly was

as calm as possible.

Then she vaulted lightly

onto her back.

But Flicka bucked her off.

Katy did not give up.

She was determined to ride
her horse.
She kept trying.
Soon, Flicka stayed calm
when Katy mounted.
Flicka trotted and cantered nicely.

Katy was thrilled.

The two of them rode out
into the night together.

It was a wonderful ride—
until Flicka spooked the herd again.

Katy's father was furious.

"I will not have her on my ranch!"
he said.

He decided to sell Flicka to the rodeo
for the wild horse race.

Katy tried to change his mind.
She argued and cried as the ranch men
loaded Flicka onto a horse trailer.
"You cannot take her!" she shouted.
But soon Flicka was gone.

Katy knew there was only one way
to get Flicka back.

She would enter the wild horse race
herself and then buy Flicka
with the winnings.

She talked her brother, Howard,
into helping.

At the rodeo, Katy disguised herself
as a boy.

Then she and Howard signed up as a
team.

They went to the corral to
choose their horse.

"We will take that black filly,"
Howard called out.

As race time neared, Howard was nervous.

He tried to talk Katy out of her plan,

but Katy was not scared at all.

Flicka had learned to trust her.

And now Katy trusted Flicka.

The race began.

It was chaos!

The horses reared and snorted and

kicked out at the cowboys.

But Katy stayed calm and

talked to Flicka.

Just as she lifted the saddle, there was

a commotion outside the ring.

Katy's parents had found out

what she was doing.

They wanted to stop the race!

Katy sprang onto Flicka's bare back.
The two of them raced right out of the
arena and away from the fairgrounds.
"I will not let them take us, girl,"
Katy said.
They galloped off into the mountains.

But the mountain lion was waiting

for them.

It growled and attacked.

Flicka fought it off,

but she was badly injured.

Katy was afraid it was the end for Flicka.

Katy's father found her and
carried her home.
Then he went out to see what
should be done about Flicka.
When Katy heard a gunshot,
she feared the worst.

But it was her father shooting
at the lion.
Flicka was a fighter.
She was not ready to die.
Katy's father carefully led
the mustang filly home.

When Katy went outside the next morning,
she was overjoyed to see Flicka
waiting for her.
This time she knew that nothing
would ever separate them again.